SPOOK SQUAD

Bats

in the

Attic

by Roger Hurn

The Isle of Fright

Vlad the Bad's Castle

Dead End Junction

The Ghost Train Railway

Ghouls' Graveyard

It's the dead centre of Otherworld!

The Wraith Pits

They really are the pits!

The Haunted Pyramid

Your mummy warned you about this place

Here There Be Dragons

Banshee Bay

Where the wind never stops howling!

They sleep in the day and fight knights!

Roger Hurn used to be an actor in 'The Exploding Trouser Company'. He has also appeared on 'The Weakest Link' on TV – and he won!

Now he spends his time writing and telling stories. His scariest and spookiest experience came when he went to an old ghost town in the Wild West of the USA. This gave him the idea for **Spook Squad**.

He hopes you enjoy reading the Spook Squad's adventures as much as he enjoyed writing them.

Spook Squad
Bats in the Attic
by Roger Hurn
Illustrated by Peter Richardson

Published by Ransom Publishing Ltd.
Radley House, 8 St. Cross Road, Winchester, Hampshire
SO23 9HX, UK
www.ransom.co.uk

ISBN   978 184167 073 7
First published in 2012

Otherworld

GOBLIN GULCH
The home of
messy eaters

FANG MOUNTAINS
You'll say 'Fangs for
nothing' if you try to
climb them

**KRAKEN
LAKE**

Swim at
your
own risk!

SPOOK CITY

THE ZOMBI RIVER

WEREWOLF WOODS
Avoid when the
moon is full!

Otherworld

Where is Otherworld?

The far side of a shadow.

Who lives there?

Ghouls, ghosts, long-leggedy beasties and things that go bump in the night.

Why do the creatures who live there come to our world?

To make mischief.

6

Rhee the Banshee answers readers' questions.

How do they get here?

> They slip through secret gateways when you're not looking.

Can humans go to Otherworld?

> Yes, but they shouldn't.

Why not?

> Because they never come back.

Why not?

> Trust me – you really **DO NOT** want to know!

7

Meet The SPOOK SQUAD

Emma

FYI: She spends her life getting hold of the wrong end of the stick.

Loves: Getting the point.

Hates: Muddy sticks.

Fact: She doesn't like vampires – she thinks they're a pain in the neck.

Roxy

FYI: Don't call her 'Ginger' – unless you want to eat your dinner through a straw.

Loves: Being a strawberry blonde.

Hates: Seeing red.

Fact: She reckons cannibal goblins are messy eaters, so she won't be joining their fang club.

Nita

FYI: This girl gets gadgets. Give her a paper clip, a rubber band, a tin can and an A4 battery and she'll rig up a gizmo that'll blow your gran's pop socks off.

Loves: Fixing things.

Hates: Fixing it – if it ain't broke.

Fact: Nita has invented ghost-proof wheels for her bike. They don't have any spooks!

Leena

FYI: If she was any sharper you could use her to slice bread.

Loves: Big words.

Hates: Small minds.

Fact: She prefers whatwolves and whenwolves to werewolves.

Aunt Rhee

FYI: Rhee's not the kind of aunt who gives you a woolly jumper for Christmas.

Loves: Walking on the wild side.

Hates: Things that go bump in the night.

Fact: Rhee is just too cool for ghouls.

Rattle

FYI: Rattle says he's a poltergeist. He thinks poltergeists are posher than ghosts.

Loves: Boo-berry pie and I-scream.

Hates: People who sneak up behind him and shout BOO!

Fact: Rattle's only happy when he's moaning.

Interview with Nita

The Spook Squad's Nita answers readers' questions.

Roxy, Emma and Leena all say you are the cleverest member of the Spook Squad. Are you?

Well, I guess so … but I don't like maths.

Why not?

Because it's got too many problems!

Do you ever get in trouble at school?

Well, I once asked my teacher if she'd ever tell me off for something I hadn't done.

What did she say?

She said of course not.

What did you say?

I said that's good because I haven't done my homework!

What's your favourite Spook Squad adventure?

Things That Go Bump in the Night.

Why?

Because we meet dragons and they are hot stuff!

The Vampire

Description: *A snappy dresser who is a pain in the neck.*

Strength: *Her bite is worse than her bark.*

Weakness: *She is a bit batty.*

Likes: *High factor sunblock.*

Dislikes: *Tooth decay.*

Favourite food: *Scream of tomato soup.*

Favourite animals: *Bloodhounds.*

Scream Scale Rating: *Fang-tastically scary!*

CREATURE
FEATURE

Chapter One

What's Cooking?

BANG!

The Spook Squad woke with a start. Something was wrong.

CRASH!

The Spook Squad leapt out of their beds and hurtled downstairs.

They burst into the kitchen. Rattle was floating over a pile of broken plates. He

held a frying pan in one ghostly hand.

'Rattle!' yelled Leena.

The poltergeist jumped. The pan flew out of his hand. The girls ducked as bits of burnt breakfast splattered everywhere. Rattle glared at the girls.

'Don't sneak up on me and then shout *Rattle*! It's bad for my nerves.'

'We didn't sneak up on you,' said Emma.

'Did, too,' said Rattle. 'You made me jump out of my skin.'

'But you're a poltergeist. You don't have a skin,' said Nita.

'Well if I did, I would have jumped out of it,' snapped the little ghost. 'Anyway, is this all the thanks I get for getting up early to make breakfast?'

Roxy peered at the burnt food on the kitchen floor. 'Yes,' she said. 'Anyway, I thought poltergeists had ghostie toasties for breakfast.'

'Oh ha ha! Anyway, this fry up isn't for me – it's for Rhee.'

'Lucky old Rhee,' said Leena. 'Hey, where is she? She can't still be asleep. The noise you made when you dropped the dishes was enough to wake the dead.'

Rattle sniffed. 'That's what she's doing – sort of. She's waking the *un*dead!'

The Spook Squad did a double take. 'She's doing *what?!!*' they chorused.

'A family of vampires has moved into the old mansion in the woods,' he said.

18

'Ooh, that's *sooo* not good news,' said
Emma.

'You're right,' agreed Rattle. 'They're a bunch of fangster gangsters, so Rhee's gone to send them back to their real home in Otherworld.'

'And where do vampires live in Otherworld?' asked Kashvi.

'On the Isle of Fright, of course,' replied Rattle.

He looked down at the pile of smashed crockery.

'Er ... you girls had better hurry up and clean up this mess before Rhee gets home from sorting out those vampires. 'Cos you'll get it in the neck if you don't!'

Then, before the Spook Squad could say a word, he vanished with a 'pop'.

Chapter Two

Spook Squad to the Rescue

'Why didn't Rhee tell us she was going to sort out a bunch of vampires?' said Emma.

'Yeah,' said Leena. 'Dealing with vampires is the kind of job we can really sink our teeth into.'

'I guess she thought the vampires would sink their teeth into us,' said Roxy.

Nita was jumping up and down by the

kitchen door.

'Come on, guys. Rhee's batty if she thinks she can sneak off hunting vampires without us!'

She charged off, with Roxy and Leena close behind.

'No, wait,' called Emma. 'First we need to ... '

But the other girls had gone. Emma looked around at the mess Rattle had made. She bent down and picked something up. She slipped it into her pocket then she ran after the others.

Chapter Three

Trapped

As Roxy, Leena and Nita ran into the woods, they saw three vampires racing up the path. The vampires' cloaks streamed out behind them as they ran.

'Get out of zee vay,' they screamed.

A few seconds later, Rhee appeared. 'Can't stop,' she gasped. 'I've got important fangs to do.' She hurtled on up the path in hot pursuit of the blood suckers.

'Do you think she'll catch them?' said Roxy.

'Well, they're neck and neck at the moment,' said Nita. 'But I guess she'll let them escape back to Otherworld.'

'So what are *we* going to do?' said Roxy.

Leena narrowed her eyes. 'Hey, let's go and check the old house out to make sure there are no vampires still lurking there.'

Roxy's face lit up in a big smile. 'Great idea, Lee. Let's do it!'

• • • • •

The gloomy old mansion looked deserted. This didn't fool the girls. They crept up to the front door. It creaked open.

Leena peered into the hallway.

'Is anybody home?' she called.

There was no answer, but a dark shape flitted across the landing at the top of the stairs.

The girls ran up the rickety stairs, but when they got to the top there was nobody there. Then Roxy noticed that the door to one of the bedrooms was slightly open. She nudged the other two and pointed. They nodded and dived in. The room was empty.

Then the door slammed shut behind them!

'For you Spook Squad ze adventure is over!' said a voice so cold it had to wear a scarf to stop itself freezing.

The girls heard the key turn in the lock. They were trapped. Then they heard a

horrible screeching sound like a hacksaw with hiccups.

'What *IS* that noise?' whispered Roxy.

Nita shrugged. 'Best guess – it's a vampire laughing.'

'Hey, remind me not to tell it a joke,' said Leena.

Chapter Four

The Vampire

Then they heard a voice call out. 'Hey, are you guys here?'

The vampire stopped laughing.

'It's Em,' said Roxy. 'And she's out there on her own with a vampire!'

Emma stood in the hallway. She couldn't see the girls anywhere. Then she saw the vampire gliding down the stairs.

'Velcome to my home,' it said. 'I do hope you'll stay for a bite.'

Emma started to back away. 'Errm ... I don't think so,' she said.

The vampire looked cross with herself. 'Duh ... I meant stay for a *bit*.'

She glided closer. 'But, of course you can have a bite as vell if you're hungry. I know I am.'

'Oh, if you're hungry have a taste of this,' said Emma. She pulled out a piece of Rattle's garlic bread from her pocket and thrust it in the vampire's face.

'YUK!' squealed the vampire. 'I HATE garlic.'

Then the sound of shouting and banging came drifting down the stairs.

'Er … I'm looking for my friends,' said Emma. 'Have you seen them?'

The vampire shook her head.

'So who's that making all the noise?' asked Emma.

The vampire smiled. Her fangs looked sharp enough to puncture car tyres.

'Ah, zat vill be my pet bloodhounds. Noisy little creatures, aren't zay?'

Emma gulped. 'I don't believe you,' she said.

'Vell believe zis,' snarled the vampire. 'It's snack attack time!'

She glided forward. Emma threw the remains of the garlic bread at her.

As the vampire ducked, Emma dodged

past her and sprinted up the stairs. She grabbed the door handle of the room where the rest of the Spook Squad were trapped, but the door was locked and the key was missing!

Chapter Five

Making a Splash

'I zink zis is vat you vant,' hissed the vampire.

Emma spun round. The vampire was right behind her. She had the key in her hand. Emma made a grab for it, but the vampire snatched it away.

'All zis exercise is making me peckish,' she said. 'So now I zink it really iz time for a bite.'

Emma turned and ran into the bathroom. The vampire followed her. Emma grabbed the toilet brush and waved it at the vampire.

'Back off, batty,' she said.

The vampire grinned. 'Oh, I'm *zo* scared,' she said.

Emma nodded. 'You should be, 'cos if you come any closer you're going to get a face full of wet, mucky bristles. And you really don't want that!'

The vampire screeched and lunged at Emma. But she stepped on a bar of soap. She skidded like an out-of-control ice skater and crashed head first into the toilet bowl! The vampire pulled and wriggled, but her head was stuck down the lavatory.

At that moment, Rhee burst into the

bathroom. She pressed the toilet flush. Immediately, the vampire began to shrink faster than a cheap vest in a hot wash. Then she vanished altogether.

'Where's she gone?' said Emma.

Rhee shrugged. 'Beats me – but she's probably feeling a bit flushed.'

Emma looked into the bowl. 'Er ... Rhee, there's a tiny little vampire doing the front crawl in the toilet. Don't you think you should rescue her?'

Rhee sighed. 'Okay – but don't expect me to give her the kiss of life!'

Emma dashed off to free the rest of the Spook Squad.

• • • • •

When the girls walked back into the bathroom, they saw a very small vampire standing in a puddle in the sink.

'Hey, I didn't know vampires were such drips,' said Roxy.

'It's a little-known fact,' said Rhee. 'Vampires shrink when wet.'

The vampire sneezed and coughed.

'I hope she's not catching a cold,' said Emma.

'Don't worry, Em,' said Leena. 'I've got some *coffin* drops I can give her!'

'But will she stay that size for good now?' asked Nita.

Rhee shook her head. 'Nope. As soon as she dries out she'll go back to her normal size – but her clothes won't!'

The Spook Squad heard a very faint sound of high-pitched squealing as the vampire jumped up and down in horror.

Rhee picked the vampire up by her shrunken dress and held it between her thumb and finger. 'Right, I'll take this vamp back to Otherworld and let her go in the main square.'

'Will she be dry by then?' asked Emma.

Rhee shook her head. 'No, but the square is hot and crowded, so she'll dry out in about two seconds flat.'

Emma frowned. 'If the vampire dries out in two seconds she'll unshrink – but her clothes won't.'

Rhee shrugged. 'So what?' she said.

'Well, she'll be stark naked in front of loads and loads of people!' said Emma.

Rhee, Leena, Nita and Roxy grinned at each other.

'That's right,' said Roxy. 'And it really couldn't happen to a nicer vampire.'

The next Spook Squad adventure is

Danger in Dead Man's Lane

It's a Scream!

Spook Squad's Scary Joke Page

What's a skeleton's favourite musical instrument?

A trom-bone!

What do you call a skeleton who won't get up in the mornings?

Lazy bones!

How do ghosts like their eggs cooked?

Terri-fried!